Time to Eat

Rockpool Children's Books
15 North Street
Marton
Warwickshire
CV23 9RJ

First published in Great Britain by Rockpool Children's Books Ltd. 2008
Text and Illustrations copyright © Stuart Trotter / Design Concept Elaine Lonergan 2007
Stuart Trotter has asserted the moral rights
to be identified as the author and illustrator of this book.

A CIP catalogue record of this book is available
from the British Library.
All rights reserved

Printed in China

rockpool
children's books

A Toddlersaurus Book

Stuart Trotter & Elaine Lonergan

Time to Eat

'Hello. My name is Steggy...

and it's time to eat.'

Mountains tumble,
what's that rumble?

It's Steggy's tummy –
hear it grumble!

Open-mouthed, snapping, hopping,

Lift the Flap

gulping popcorn
as it's popping!

When the ground shakes and quakes...

Lift the Flap

his breakfast flakes!

It's Steggy crunching

Splat! One in the eye,
'Thanks a bunch,'

As Steggy munches at his lunch!

'Gurgle, gurgle, gulp and slurp!'

After fun eating,

it's now bathtime

in Toddlersaurus land.....

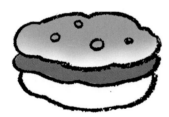

but that's

another story!

'Good bye!'